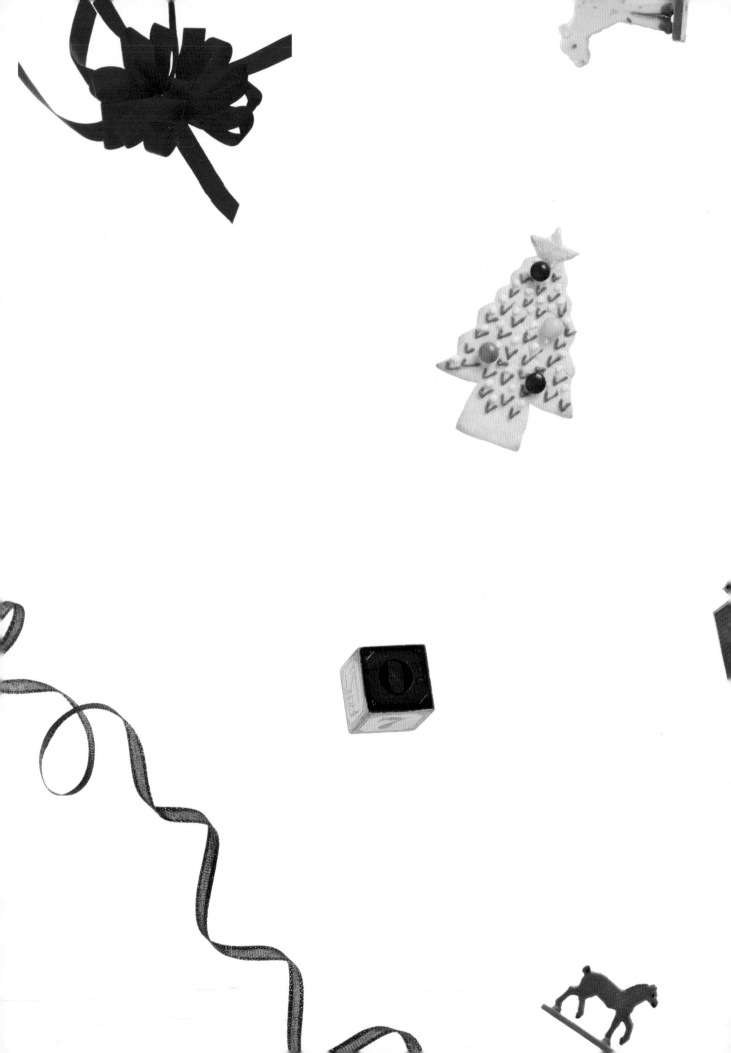

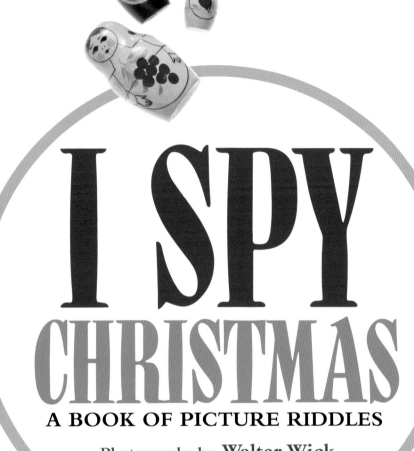

I SPY
CHRISTMAS
A BOOK OF PICTURE RIDDLES

Photographs by **Walter Wick**
Riddles by **Jean Marzollo**

With new bonus challenges by
Dan Marzollo and **Dave Marzollo**

cartwheel books™

An imprint of Scholastic Inc.
New York

For my parents, Betty and Peter Wick
W.W.

Book design by Carol Devine Carson

Text copyright © 1992 by Jean Marzollo
Illustrations and photographs copyright © 1992 by Walter Wick
Bonus challenges copyright © 2019 by Dan Marzollo and Dave Marzollo

Library of Congress Cataloging-in-Publication Data available
ISBN 978-1-338-33258-2
10 9 8 7 6 5 4 3 2   20 21 22 23
Printed in China   62
This edition first printing, September 2019

TABLE OF CONTENTS

....

Picture riddles fill this book;
Turn the pages! Take a look!

Use your mind, use your eye;
Read the rhymes and play I SPY!

....

I spy a clock, a bumpy green pickle,
Santa on a sleigh and a face on a nickel;

A frog on a leaf, a chubby teddy bear,
Black and white keys, and a yellow-red pear.

I spy a horse and three glitter shells,
A five-pointed star, and two silver bells;

One golden ring, a little white cat,
A swan and a bear and a thimble hat.

I spy a snowman, three hens in a row,
A drumstick, a rabbit, a small yellow bow;

An almond, a magnet, a seagull, a chick,
A hammer, five cents, and a wooden toothpick.

I spy a jingle bell, two birds of blue,
A bunny, a star, and Santa's red shoe;

An old-fashioned key, two small striped stones,
A red shoelace, and seven pinecones.

I spy a wagon, five sleds, and a drum,
A smart ladybug, and a stick of gum;

Two snowy mittens, three pairs of gloves,
A monkey named Socks, and two turtledoves.

I spy a house, a drum, and a clock,
Three fat pigs, and a squirrel-tail sock;

A string of lights, a belt with a B,
A candy cane, and a broken tree.

I spy a thimble, four birds of red,
Two fuzzy chickens, a gold-trimmed sled;

Three paper clips, an ornament house,
A bottle of glue, and a nutty brown mouse.

I spy a goose, a cat lying down,
A paintbrush, an acorn, a chick, and a clown;

A buffalo nickel, a bird on a block,
Six musical bears, and a key for a lock.

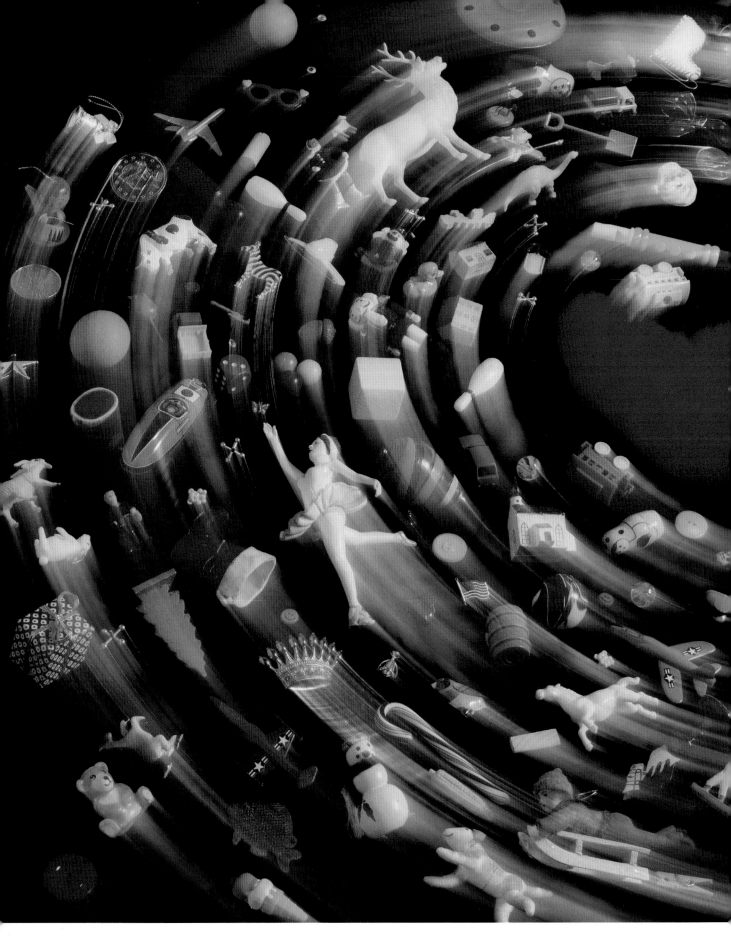

I spy a checker, three candy canes,
A little yellow chick, and seven airplanes;

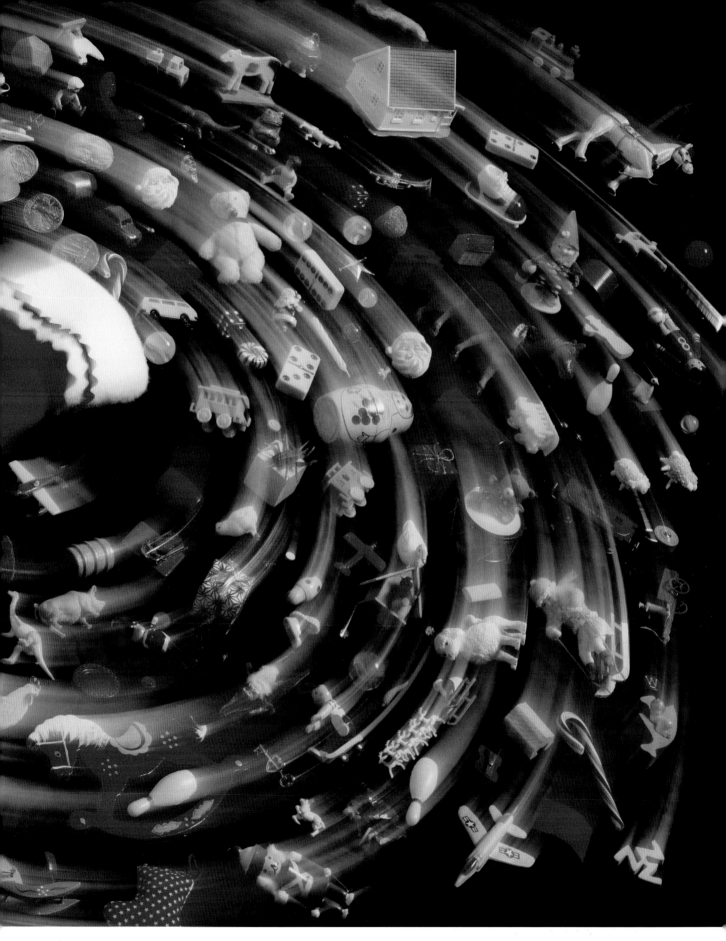

A pink clothespin, a steeple on a church,
One toy top, and a bird on a perch.

I spy a fish, a brown hatband,
A horse, a cow, and a pointing hand;

A teapot pin, a bell-ringing bear,
A tiny birdhouse, and Santa in a chair.

I spy an ice cube, a little twist of lime,
A carrot for a nose, a slim silver dime;

A hatchet at work, a bottle, and a key,
A pinecone, a plane, and a Christmas tree.

I spy a rooster, a Santa with a cane,
The shadow of a star, a car for a train;

Two fancy coaches, a ribbon of blue,
Some musical notes, and JOY 2 U, too.

I spy a glove, a horse, and a gate,
A silver coin, the shadow of a skate;

A shovel, a lamb, a Christmas tree light,
Five jacks, and a dove in the dark silent night.

BONUS CHALLENGES

by **Dan Marzollo** and **Dave Marzollo**

"Find Me" Riddle

I'm on every page with a wand that's gold,
I'm Santa's _____; I'm small but old.

There are still more riddles for you to complete.
Here is a challenge for readers to beat!

Every picture has a new set of clues.
Can you pick the right page to choose?

I spy a marble, a pinecone, a bow,
A dove, a drum, and a cup filled with snow.

I spy a gear, a pickup truck,
A puzzle piece, and a little white duck.

I spy a plaid heart, a shiny metal cat,
A solid gold eye, and a bear in Santa's hat.

I spy a bracelet, a spool of thread,
An angel on a tree, and a goat that's red.

I spy an elephant, a spiral shell,
An angel, a ladybug, and a bell.

I spy three angels, a tiny white tree,
Two sheep, an accordion, and a block turkey.

I spy a teacup, a reindeer's eye,
A tag, a top, and a single die.

I spy a zebra, a penguin, a parrot,
A silver bell, a van, and a carrot.

I spy a flashlight, two little cars,
A ballerina bear, and two blue stars.

I spy a domino, balloons on a string,
A lamb lying down, a vest, and a spring.

I spy a gold coin, a mitten that's green,
A red top hat, and a musical scene.

I spy antlers, curly blue hair,
A purple star, and a metal bear.

I spy a ballerina, a red gummy O,
Unwrapped foil, and a flake of snow.

Write Your Own Picture Riddles

There are many more hidden objects and many more
possibilities for riddles in this book. Write some rhyming
picture riddles yourself, and try them out with friends.

Special Acknowledgments

First of all, thank you to Grace Maccarone, Bernette Ford, Jean Feiwel, Barbara Marcus, Edie Weinberg, John Illingworth, and Lenora Todaro. Also, we would like to thank all the people at Scholastic who have supported the I Spy books.

A heartfelt thanks to our agent, Molly Friedrich of The Aaron M. Priest Literary Agency, for her wit, wisdom, and willingness to solve problems creatively and thoroughly.

We'd like to thank artists Missy Stevens and Tommy Simpson for letting us use their extraordinary collections of antique teddy bears, antique ornaments, and handcrafted Christmas decorations.

And finally, thank you to Dora Jonassen for the cookies, Evan G. Hughes for the evergreens, Christopher M. Hayes and Linda Bayette for help with "Santa's Workshop," Verde Antiques for various props in "Window Shopping," Katherine O'Donnell and Marianne Alibozak for their photo assistance, and Linda Cheverton-Wick for her superb artistic eye.

Walter Wick and Jean Marzollo

Walter Wick is the award-winning photographer of the I Spy series as well as the author and photographer of the bestselling Can You See What I See? series. His other books include *A Ray of Light: A Book of Science and Wonder* and *A Drop of Water: A Book of Science and Wonder*. He has created photographs for books, magazines, and newspapers. Walter's photographs have been featured in museums around the United States. He lives with his wife, Linda, in Miami Beach, Florida.

More information about Walter Wick is available at walterwick.com and scholastic.com/canyouseewhatisee.

Jean Marzollo was the author of over a hundred books, including the bestselling I Spy series; *Help Me Learn Numbers 0-20*; *Help Me Learn Addition*; *Help Me Learn Subtraction*; and *I Am Water*; as well as books for parents and teachers, such as *The New Kindergarten*. Her sons, Dan and Dave, helped Jean write some of the newer I Spy books. Jean made sure that every riddle in every I Spy book was rich with concrete words that children could understand and that those words were set in an inviting pattern of rhythm and rhyme. For more information, go to scholastic.com/ispy.

Carol Devine Carson, the book designer, has designed covers for books by John Updike, Joan Didion, Alice Munro, and many more. For nineteen years, Marzollo and Carson produced Scholastic's kindergarten magazine, *Let's Find Out*.